THIS WALKER BOOK BELONGS TO:

_____

_____

_____

_____

For Thomas, Katie and David

First published 1989 by Lutterworth Press
by whose permission the present edition is published.
This edition published 1991 by Walker Books Ltd
87 Vauxhall Walk, London SE11 5HJ

© 1989 Bert Kitchen

Printed and bound in Hong Kong by
Dai Nippon Printing Co. (HK) Ltd

British Library Cataloguing in Publication Data
Kitchen, Bert
Tenrec's twigs.
I. Title
823'.914 [J]
ISBN 0-7445-1793-1

TENREC'S TWIGS

BERT KITCHEN

WALKER BOOKS

LONDON

As the sun rose over the hill, Tenrec popped his head out of his burrow and sniffed the fresh morning air.

The weather was dry and bright, just right for building. He snuffled along until he came to the place where he had gathered a pile of twigs the day before.

He walked around the twigs several times, humming happily. Then he began to build.

He pushed thick twigs into the ground in a circle, and rested more twigs on these. Then he chose twigs that seemed springy and bendy, and wove them in and out, stepping back from time to time to see how the shape was coming along.

Then Old Warthog came by. He could be grumpy at the best of times, but today he was feeling particularly miserable. He plonked his hoof right on the side of Tenrec's twig building.

"Useless! A waste of time!" he grumbled. "Ask any of the other animals."

And he went on his way.

Tenrec was upset. Useless, he thought. A waste of time? He decided he would ask some of the other animals.

Tenrec spied Grey Parrot on a branch above him. Before he could even ask the question, Grey Parrot squawked, "Useless! Useless! A waste of time."

"I haven't even asked you the question," Tenrec said. Then he realized that Grey Parrot had overheard Old Warthog. He was simply repeating what he had heard.

"I'll ask someone else," Tenrec said to himself. Soon he came across Giant Anteater. He asked him what he thought of his twigs.

"Strange as it seems," said Anteater, "although I do have a long nose, I don't really like poking it into other creatures' business. So I wouldn't like to say. But I have just seen Pangolin hanging about. Why not ask him?"

Tenrec found Pangolin hanging by his tail from a high branch. To get closer Tenrec quickly made a small twig platform and asked him his question.

But Pangolin was so wrapped up in himself and his own thoughts, he could not even be bothered to try to understand. "Twigs? Buildings, Tenrec?" he said in an absent-minded voice.

Tenrec was feeling no happier. Then he spotted Giraffe munching leaves way up in the trees above him. It seemed as though Giraffe's head were in the clouds. Tenrec tapped him on the hoof to get his attention.

"Giraffe, I don't know if you have noticed my little twig buildings," Tenrec asked politely, "but do you think I should stop building them?"

Giraffe bent down, "I've never noticed your twigs, Tenrec, so I have no feeling for or against them." With that he straightened up and his head disappeared into the leaves again.

J ust then Tenrec saw Golden Mole shuffling along, looking for food. Surely he will see things my way, thought Tenrec. So he said to Mole, "Do you think I am foolish to make my twig buildings?"

"I spend most of my time underground in the dark, Tenrec. I can see little or nothing out here. I am afraid I know nothing about your buildings."

Just as Mole finished speaking, Adjutant Stork came strutting along. Tenrec put his question to the tall bird.

Adjutant Stork puffed out his chest, looking very important. "Well," he said, "in my opinion . . . as a matter of fact . . . perhaps . . ." but, overcome by his own importance, he completely forgot the question and began to strut away.

Tenrec was beginning to lose heart when he came upon Two-Toed Sloth hanging sleepily from the bough of a tree. "Sloth," he said, "Do you think I should stop building my twigs? Warthog says there is no use for them."

Now Sloth was extremely slow. Finally he said, "Ask me again tomorrow, Tenrec, or better still next week (yawn) . . . It is such a difficult question (yawn) that I need plenty of time (yawn) in order to . . ." Before Sloth could finish the sentence he had fallen asleep.

Who else could Tenrec ask? Did nobody care about his twigs? Then Tenrec remembered Milky Eagle Owl. He made his way to Owl's perching place where he knew the bird spent many hours just sitting and thinking.

"Please, Owl," he asked, "do you think my twig-building is useless and a waste of time?"

Owl closed his eyes for several seconds, then said, "Hmmm, I find your twig building very interesting, Tenrec. You seem very happy when you are building and you certainly do not bother me, hmmm, or anyone else. In fact you may inspire others to build. My advice is to continue building!"

Now Tenrec had his answer. Humming happily, he went back to his building and pushed another twig into the ground.

ANIMALS IN THE STORY
in order of appearance

All the animals in this story exist, even though they may
look too weird and wonderful to be true. Most of them
come from central and southern Africa.

The main character in this story is a **Streaked Tenrec**.
Tenrecs are small creatures, resembling something between
a shrew and a hedgehog and are found only on the island of
Madagascar. Tenrecs are inquisitive, tenacious little animals,
and are very active. Their habitat is being destroyed, but
they have not yet been declared a protected species as some
of the larger animals from that part of the world have been.
Without protection they may soon become extinct.

Warthogs get their name from the two large warts or
protuberances they have on each side of their head. The old,
darker boars are usually loners.

The **African Grey Parrot** is renowned for its
outstanding ability to mimic the human voice. Parrots are
known to live up to 50 years, sometimes even longer.

The **Giant Anteater**, as its name suggests, feeds on ants
and termites. With its four strong claws on its forelegs the
anteater rips open the muddy walls of nests. It then inserts its
long tongue, which is covered in sticky saliva so that the
insects stick to it.

The **Small-scaled Pangolin** in this story is one of
several types of pangolin. Using their long tails pangolins
will spend much of their time climbing trees. They too have
long and sticky tongues to help them catch their food.

The **Giraffe** is one of the tallest animals and feeds on
leaves and fruit from the top of acacia and thorn trees.
When drinking, the giraffe has to splay its front legs in order
to stoop down.

The **Golden Mole** spends much of its time underground,
and its eyes are almost lost now, being covered with hairy
skin. Golden moles have a sense of touch which they use
when looking for food, and a strong sense of smell which
they use for finding new burrows, foraging for food and
seeking partners for breeding.

The **Marabou "Adjutant" Stork** acquired its name
because of its pompous measured walk which reminded
British colonial troops of adjutant officers. Although
ungainly when on the ground adjutant storks fly well and
can soar like vultures.

The **Two-toed Sloth** is very inactive and sluggish in its movements. Awkward on the ground, sloths spend most of their life in trees, suspended by means of powerful, hooked claws. Sloths eat, sleep and even give birth while hanging upside-down from the branches of trees.

The **Milky Eagle Owl** like many other owls, hunts at twilight. By day these owls perch on rocks or trees camouflaged by their plumage. They sit with eyes almost closed, but the slightest noise arouses them. The owl has been associated with wisdom since ancient times.

MORE WALKER PAPERBACKS
For You to Enjoy

ANIMAL ALPHABET / ANIMAL NUMBERS
by Bert Kitchen

"Very beautiful… In the category of 'collectable classics'… As much for adults as for children." *Books for Keeps*

Animal Alphabet   0-7445-1776-1   £3.99
Animal Numbers   0-7445-1780-X   £3.99

LARGE AS LIFE ANIMALS
by Joanna Cole
illustrated by Kenneth Lilly

In this stunning natural history book, each picture shows an animal at its actual size and in its normal habitat. There's a short, lively text with more detailed natural history notes at the back.

"Finely detailed double-page paintings… My nine-year-old child gives them a hundred marks out of ten, and I agree."
Andy Martin, BBC Wildlife

0-7445-2076-2   £5.99